ACOUSTIC SHADOWS

Essays from a Standing Pianist

JACK KOHL

THE PAUKTAUG PRESS

Pauktaug, New York

Published by:
The Pauktaug Press
Pauktaug, New York

Copyright © 2024 by Jack Kohl

ISBN: 979-8-218-40428-4

"Praise of God in Solitude" originally ran
in *The Continental Literary Magazine.*

Cover illustration:
Freiman Stoltzfus • www.freimanstoltzfus.com

Interior design:
Gary A. Rosenberg • www.thebookcouple.com

Printed in the United States of America

Contents

OTHER TITLES BY JACK KOHL

Foreword

by David Dubal

Franz Liszt said that some music comes to you, and to other music you must go to it. This is certainly true of literature, and it is certainly true of the writing of Jack Kohl, who can be recondite but never thorny. His is a beguiling style. Kohl's essays and novels always end in stylish prose. But once you come to him wholeheartedly you will stay with him. All subjects written by Mr. Kohl are chromatic and bejeweled and can be appreciated by those who still have the energy to go to him.

Although Mr. Kohl has great knowledge of the classics in both literature and as a concert pianist (the literature of the keyboard), he is, however, never a mere specialist, but an admiring generalist even within far-flung fields. For me this can hold the essence of a friendship, and in this day and age to talk to one about many things seems quite wonderful. I first met Jack as a concert pianist who adores that great literature of the piano. I knew he had travailed within the gigantic scope of Charles Ives' *Concord, Mass.* Sonata (one of the difficult works of the piano literature of all centuries). I remember a couple seasons back, in my piano class in New York City, where Mr. Kohl played each movement as we detailed for many this challenging score—*Emerson* being the huge opening movement. And as with the other movements, we talked to the audience about the composition. There is much prejudice about anything difficult. But on those days we converted some people at least into the Ivesian fields.

So I have established here that the author of these essays in *Acoustic Shadows* brings to his writing a deep tactile understanding through his sensitive hearing—that in music, the piano, even in the hidden gardens of the literature, Jack Kohl's sensibility is stirred by the immortal black and white keyboard, the most magnificent monochrome ever created, and through the transcendence of music that is no longer esoteric but still difficult to encounter in length and spirit.

A musician and a writer of the quality and depth of Mr. Kohl naturally comes through many tributaries, and if you read his work you will know him as lover of sweet tea and one of the very serious joggers and observers of Nature.

The reader will find remarkable things in these essays without having to play piano himself. If Kohl plays it or does not play it, the instrument permeates his existence in many areas of life, hence his beguiling subtitle: *Essays from a Standing Pianist* for his three volumes of essays. There are many allusions to personal realities in Kohl's imaginative world. For example, who else would think of walking a dog in his study on the Liszt Sonata, as Kohl does in the first essay in the book *Bone Over Ivory*? Or would you imagine connecting the Circle of Fifths to a circular trail in the forest, as is well-explained in his second essay book *From the Windows of Diligence*? Even the essay "Trapestry" (in the present volume) is a story of unrequited romance; here you will find both the touch of Woman and of the keyboard.

Do not be frightened off by the symbolic. Here we have prose that always represents the concrete and the human. The writer gives the reader his full sway of his imaginative scope.

Acoustic Shadow

I submit that the topography of the Village of Northport, Long Island, New York, with complements from traces of a vanished Gilded Age, reveal one of the most astounding instances of Acoustic Shadow known to the author—more impressive to me than, say, the great example given by the Battle of Gettysburg: the sound of which faded over the Pennsylvania countryside but revealed itself with great clarity once more to the city of Pittsburgh, almost two-hundred miles away.

Here, from where I write to you now (yet not at a piano, mind) at an old rolltop desk on the second floor of a house (a house in which I have lived all of my life) that looks down from the hilly end of a dead-street onto Northport Harbor, I have been immersed for a half-century in the guidance of a singular Acoustic Shadow and have reached thereby my apotheosis as a pianist, as a Standing Pianist, if you will.

Other sounds evocative of village life reach me here at my desk on the hilltop, but they are degraded in volume over (and by) the course of their direct journey to my ear. As strong as is the fire siren atop Ocean Avenue Elementary School (on a hilltop a mile from where I write), it is only a faint reminder of my schooldays when I hear it here at home. Sounding in complement yet superior authority to the school's siren is the siren atop the Village Firehouse. Its power is such that I have seen visitors jump with surprise when it is sounded, even when it is used for only a short blast to mark noon. Yet here on my hilltop, which is closer to the firehouse than to the school, the volume of the former's siren is rendered into a companionable and reassuring horn, even over the short crow's flight it has to travel here to my desk.

On holidays one can hear, too, from here (though muted, as well) the roll-offs of the Northport High School Marching Band's drums, marking the transitions within its medleys. The pattern of those roll-offs are as fixed as the sirens—they have not changed at all in my lifetime—and thus from a distance it suggests that even classmates of mine who have passed away are still there, below on Main Street, marching in place until the veterans preceding them have completed laying laurels at the monuments. Even in the hushed and gentle chatter preceding autumn funerals, remembrance of those roll-offs has allowed me, while waiting for the arrival of the priest, to pass the time with classmates I hardly knew.

Again, I am a pianist, and thus I never marched with the band. Yet by watching the band pass I formed the impression that mystic geologic forces from the Gilded Age formed the canyon of this Main Street, USA, as much as any act of masonry. If Grand Canyons are carved by millions of years of a river's patriotism, then Northport's Main Street seemed carved to me as from the great erosive sweep of a thousand past Sousa parades. But, alas, this small canyon is at its terminal depth now, for the river of Main Street's parades has been reduced to an ineffectual rill, by marching bands that play trickling, rootless, pop songs in place of the former rapids that flowed with the power of Civil Religion.

Main Street's buildings—looking from top to bottom—reflect the fossil analogy of what I say: the tops still retain the grand, ponderous chauvinism of a late nineteenth-century stonework, rich with remembered hope and doubtlessness; but the

windows and doors and interiors at street level—
the most recent, but, at last, least impressed layers
—change only from the splashes and detritus of the
pop songs' whims. But, again, the present stream is
too weak to deepen further the base of the canyon.

So I look up to its rim on my present walks,
with a pining for a late nineteenth-century patina
held within the stones' grip, a patina that deep ret-
rospection exalts—not just for a time between the
passing of the frontier and the arrival of the motor
car (a time cast as if in a faded, amber, light, as
that of an antique photograph), but that species
of patina (as one hears in the whiff of a Charles
Ives parlor song quotation or in lines of Booth
Tarkington: "it has gone, like the all-day picnic in
the woods, and like that prettiest of all vanished
customs, the serenade"), a patina that creates a
gloriously productive paradox—an intensity of
patina through which radiates something not only
irretrievable but, as well, a species of Platonism, a
method for animating a Universal present.

But perhaps the great, formative, river of the
past of which I speak did not so much run dry as
it is held behind some sort of dam, as it seems
an accumulated vapor from that figurative aquifer

seems now to finish the parade route and land upon the Village Bandshell on midweek summer nights, in the Village Park adjacent to Northport's Harbor. It is from there that the great Acoustic Shadow of which I write originates before making its way to me. There almost seems a balance of the occult and the actual when I invoke a mythological precipitation targeting the bandshell, for among my earliest memories of my native village is one of seeking refuge on that covered bandshell during an unexpected and very powerful rainstorm. I was three years old, and I remember marching in sudden depths. My mother and an aunt aimed for the bandshell, and there we were stranded. Yet a Village Police car plowed through the water like a canoe, even leaving the beginning of a wake, and approached the bandshell. The officer beckoned for us to descend its stairs and to get in the patrol car. I remember how slick the rear seat seemed with the rain. We were driven home. The Bandshell and its surrounding park had been built on former shipyard grounds, and I wonder if the rains that often pool about the bandshell come not only to remind one of the land's original use, but so that I might discover that what is built now on the bandshell is still to be launched onto the harbor, yet bound at last for the most personal coordinates.

A year after the great rainstorm I graduated (whilst wearing a little, navy-blue sailor's suit) from the Village Pre-School, in a ceremony held in front of that bandshell. In Jr. High School I stood behind a pitiable electronic keyboard (as part of the school's jazz ensemble) in almost the exact same spot in which I had sat and waited for my name to be called during the Pre-School's commencement observation. But whereas I was able to grasp my diploma when it was offered, my principal memory of the Jr. High School concert is of the printed pages being carried away from my music stand by a spring wind.

Thus I have never had cause to be part of any event held on the deck of the bandshell. Yet during late autumn evenings, when the park is empty, I sometimes climb its steps and stand again where I had once been sheltered from the rain. From there I look back on the Village's Green, rendered a mysterious blue in the autumn evening's light, and I recall the Green as it appeared to me (dotted with blankets, and with lighted cigarettes moving slowly just above, the latter in lazy and envious complement to the bandleader's baton) when I first had cause as a little boy, from that close range, to hear the Sousa pour forth from under the Bandshell under Mr. Kruger's leadership.

When I stand on that empty deck, I cannot quite see up into the hills of my home to the southeast, where the Acoustic Shadow will go. The Village Christmas tree blocks that view, for it stands between the Bandshell and the exit to the park. Yet the Christmas Tree is hardly the only baffle responsible for muting the band as one leaves the park whilst the Sousa is still sounding. I would suggest that the sound of the band, like the sounds of the two fire sirens I describe above, simply begins to diminish in power as it makes its way through the village and up into the hills. But either because it has such less brute force than the sirens, or because some other suggestive power is at play in its case, one cannot help noticing that the band's sound seems almost to vanish altogether after entering the village, or in making one's way south along the long street that parallels the harbor's edge and leads to the bottom of the hill on which I live. Does the stream of the Sousa reject something in the modern incarnation of the village? Or does the impeding space filter out some impurity from the source and compel its unadulterated form to travel by another avenue: the harbor?

Again, upon reaching the base of my home's hill, at the intersection where begins the principal east-bound climb of my dead-end street, there is almost no trace of the band's sound, even as they continue to perform at less than a quarter mile's distance away; and on the western side of the intersection, a last, very small, bit of my street abuts the harbor's edge with a little set of derelict wooden steps that lead down to the mud of low tide. This makes my street, in effect, an avenue with two dead-ends—yet, as I have hinted, both with miraculous aural afterlives waiting beyond the ostensible termini.

Before I begin the climb of my hill from the intersection, I recall often that many years ago my family's first cat, answering some irresistible call of her final wasting phase, made her way, in two instances, to a dinghy moored at the base of the little wooden stairway. In both cases, after a sighting by a neighbor, I retrieved our cat from the dinghy—where she sat upright and looked toward the Centerport shoreline across the harbor; or, stared perhaps, to some undetermined point on the intervening water during a fog (when distant prospects are removed, when usually empty spaces of mere transparency and transition for the body and eye become as quadrants, chambers, upon which focus and parameters may be imposed)—and I felt in both cases that I had done right in bringing her home; now I wonder if I meddled.

For when one has completed, say, only twenty yards of the climb up the hilly street from the quiet intersection—as one comes parallel with a small, level garden (where long ago a neighbor glazed that tiny plane in winter into a small ice rink for children), the profound unveiling of the Acoustic Shadow begins: for as one walks still farther away from the Bandshell and climbs toward the domain of its Shadow, one walks toward a sound of such intensity that it rivals its source—no, almost bests the power and presence of the originating actuality. Thus, one walks as if toward an actuality with no source, no body, and no ultimate location; yet since one walks toward the more potent realization, and though it is without a definitive location, it still has an approximate though unspoilable place. Where is the air from which such a miracle can draw its breath for brass? Has there ever been

9

greater evidence that the Stars and Stripes are to last forever?

This Shadow intensifies as one reaches the driveway of my home, and I must qualify the virtue of its power when it is subjected to abuse. The Shadow admits trespassers when, during nights of late summer, boorish rock bands play on the bandshell, and the watery conduit of the harbor also carries astonishingly realized blunders and intrusions from wedding receptions of the Centerport Yacht Club on the opposite shore. So strange to me it is that these ugly noises of trespass from the latter are part of the routine that immediately succeeds a putatively holy alliance! I am not invited to the formal part of the ceremony, but I am a compulsory guest to its gruesome aftermath: a recital as if given by chainsaws. I take no exception to the nightly report of the same Yacht Club's evening cannon; and I relish the occasional sound of the railroad horn that comes, as well, via the Shadow's conduit of the harbor (acting as the reliable harbinger of rain on succeeding days), and, too, the warm cheers of an unseen crowd that come to me in early December when the Village Christmas tree is lighted for the first time—for all these sounds carry with them the foundations of necessity. Yet I concede that many may retort to my earlier objections by saying: One man's intruder is another man's missionary.

But one evening I emerged from the insulated silence of my car into the presence of a trespasser in my driveway. The Shadow of the Centerport Yacht Club's wedding band was so intense that for a moment I took the sound to be coming from within my home. But though I quickly identified the intruder as a passenger of the Shadow's conduit, I resolved that night to call the police.

The patrol car duly arrived. With an exasperated wave of my hand I pointed to the almost immediate, solid presence of an intruder who originated from nearly a mile away (an intruder likely unheard, however, by anyone a half-mile away).

"What do you want me to do?" asked the policeman. "I can't go over there and shut them down. It might be different if it were after hours and you were sleeping."

I wanted to make a combative reply: "So only my sleep is sacred?" But I did not say that.

I realized that I had to pay the price of one who dreams while awake. The officer left, for he could not pin a ticket onto the Shadow or rescue me from that kind of Bandshell. My temper eased as I realized that I could level no charge against an intruder who is inadvertently swept up into the ultimately higher purpose of God's best ventriloquism. And when the last hackneyed noises of the wedding party faded, I looked at the side of my house and found that the Shadow of the cover band had left no lasting marks—no more than the school marching band's new medleys have any, lasting, geological effect on the first-floor storefronts on Main Street.

So I climb to the highest floor of my home on summer nights, when the Shadow is set to bring the Sousa, and I wait at this very desk. Before the music comes, the Shadow brings me the gentle clinks of the buoys of the harbor, of the bobbing sounds from the ostensibly open space into which long ago my cat had stared. All matter begins to seem as formless as a harbor then—all objects revealed then, as the pianist Alfred Brendel has observed, "to act like those whom Busoni accused of treating the pedal 'in much the same way as they might try to force air and water into geometric shapes.'"

The eerie immediacy of the buoys' sound, clinking via the Shadow as if in my very chamber, thus renders everything in my solid midst (including my very person) as if into the formlessness of water, as if into disembodied abstraction—the Acoustic Shadow of the buoys not an intruder but as a missionary to me. Thus, at last, only the mechanistic, the material, part of my mind is left to me, that material as if a final proxy of the Gilded Age stone atop Main Street's canyon, onto which the succeeding waves from the Bandshell can carve their sculptures. And I rise, otherwise disembodied, a Standing Pianist, one bound to no instrument—a Platonist caryatid with universal concerns, yet with a crown chiseled by Sousa.

I stand before this desk in a perfect realization of "The Stars and Stripes Forever"—yet standing here free of all the trappings, materials, and instruments, of the musical art; standing in the dead center of a perfect aural realization of the band, yet not standing in the midst of other players nor performing myself, though a threadbare gap in the Shadow permits me a sense of performer's agency: to insert in my mind's ear the piccolo solo that fell as tret and tare over the sea. Surely this effect teaches a certain kind of man to keep his beloved forever at a distance whilst at the same time he courts her and pines for her with complete focus. A Standing Pianist who walks in the midst of such a Shadow is as a spirit who is always being restored to his man, yet is as a man who is always being rendered into his spirit, all this in a breathtaking immediacy of negligible segue.

America's Greatest Family: The O'Lanterns

With increasing frequency during the course of my lifetime's Octobers I have noticed a paradox developing in the Halloween decorations of my neighbors here in the American northeast. They often erect summaries, representations, miniaturizations, of what their own yards, homes, and neighborhoods present best already, yet the displays are, of course, smaller and humbler than the actuality. I have seen faux-cemeteries built on properties next to actual graveyards; as well as immense, vinyl, imitation jack-o'-lanterns pinned to the ground next to rows of weighty, uncarved, pumpkins; and I have seen pudgy, inflatable, animated dioramas depicting scenes of weathered Gothic houses, these dioramas displayed on New England streets that boast the very same scenes in original under moonlight. This phenomenon may appear less odd in more arid or tropical parts of the United States, but here in the northeast the paradox of such displays exceeds the transgression of placing a lighted plastic snowman in a yard covered in snow—for lighted plastic snowmen have earned a place of five-and-dime remembrance outside of their original roles. But, again, when does a northeast autumn ever fail to present in perfected actuality what meek, parenthetical, imitations cannot? One may as well present postcards of famous paintings in the corners of the frames of those very paintings, or carry around a photo of oneself on one's neck at a social function. Yet, alas, the ID card has made the absurdity of the latter a commonplace.

On the final day of October, all that is required in the yards of northeastern towns is a single jack-o'-lantern. But perhaps the flabby, paradoxical labors of my secular neighbors are to be pardoned, for the even greater and more concentrated paradox presented by a single, lighted, and putatively secular jack-o'-lantern suggests layers of immortal essence and beauty perhaps too great to bear for a society equipped only for recognizing great symbols by avoiding them.

The paradox suggested by the jack-o'-lantern: that while excessive and enormous contemporary yard decorations fail to summarize what their immediate surroundings better represent, the diminutive jack-o'-lantern—seemingly but a small component of its greater autumn setting—summarizes infinitely more than its surroundings. Each year I ask a jack-o'-lantern to account for this paradox, and I endeavor to wrest answers from him that I can never compel. To stare into a face that one must confront but that will not answer is the hardest of tasks. Perhaps we most personify the most unpersonifiable things because it seems the only way to coax the unknowable from them, but from first to last, the jack-o'-lantern himself never appears to relinquish intimations of personality.

The pumpkin, even before carving, preserves the earliest representations many of us make of ourselves. In kindergarten, whilst wrestling with my first attempts at drawing the human form, I looked across to my classmate Joshua's work and was impressed by his bodiless portraits—arms and legs, as thin as vines, attached directly to heads. And in a recent October, when I took away the lone pumpkin I bought from a sale in a churchyard and placed it in the front passenger seat of my car, the church volunteer suggested in humorless earnest that I buckle *him* up. I did not heed the advice, but after

I drove several blocks the seatbelt alarm would not cease sounding. I was compelled to pull over and acknowledge a second passenger. One is never permitted to feel alone in a pumpkin's presence.

I am always fascinated by the very fine, silt-like traces of mud that remain affixed in the wrinkled lines of longitude on most pumpkins I select for interrogation. Contact with such dirt never leaves me feeling unclean, even when it remains on my hands as I eat. Perhaps this is as the encrusted sleep that forms in the eyes of those born without eyes, and cleaning the sleep from the eyes of an infant rarely seems unsanitary. This silt is also common on the sides of pumpkins, in the scars that form from the way they have lain through growth. These scars are as the bedhead marks that impress themselves into our own skin and remain briefly on the faces of those who must rush from bed—as if dreams leave marks from the waffle iron from the Land of Nod. But such marks do not disappear from pumpkins after they are harvested from their dusty beds. Their bedhead marks are indelible. This suggests that a pumpkin never wakes up in life. Is he sleeping even when he is at his end, when he is carved? All during autumn one sees in a pumpkin's face the last impression of his long summer dream. We cut our own impressions into his skin so that we may coax him to speak his dreams; one then lights the candle in the jack-o'-lantern to compel him further. But we remain, at last, as powerless as the executioner by fire of the martyr. By their stoic silence, the martyr, along with the pumpkin, only seem to goad one to further means of torture. Yet no poet will share his dreams by extortion.

When fire in the pumpkin fails, we place their kind in the fire. Our aims then seem no better than November squirrels. But we sense that if we cannot compel the dreamer to speak we will learn the dream by eating the dreamer. We eat the pie in the hope of planting a parthenogenetic seed within, more fierce perhaps than any native germ, to depose the dreams we already hold that have not the mettle to explode. Yet we plant the wrong seeds in the wrong wombs when we hope for greater feats from our heirs than ourselves. Do pumpkins try this at times, as well? In one instance in my life, I found a germinating seed in a pumpkin only moments after I cut into its top.

Even an unceremonious deterioration leaves the pumpkin silent; no indignity compels. Humanity takes pains to arrange for the reverential disposal of its dead; pumpkins, however, begin the process of cremation on the night of their apotheosis. Then the potbellied squirrels, the deer, the childish vandals, the car tires of November design the pumpkin's scattered mausoleums, and I find I must pay my respects *everywhere*, yet without the melancholy that attends seeing Christmas trees consigned to January roadsides. The village becomes an open casket of shattered remains, of good-humored fragments that the undertaker's art could never improve. The earliest hour of November is as the smokey, dark minute after a fireworks display; November 1st is as a July 5th to jack-o'-lanterns. I comb the streets and examine the unspent candles. Fossilized breezes in the wax document the influence of the lost jack-o'-lanterns' faces, but only a record of the breaths they drew and nothing of outgoing words. I save the unspent candles, yet I achieve the same results notwithstanding the insertion of old or new in the following year.

Sometimes I find a dead insect encased in the cooled wax—one so enchanted by flickering images that it perished as one who would attempt to squeeze through the little window fronting a theater's projection room. However, I have yet to find in the wax any of the crickets that sing the Farewell Symphony of cooling October. Who is the Haydn behind it all? Might one locate the last singer in that diminishing ensemble, the final ventriloquist for the silent jack-o'-lanterns? After giving the mortal puff to the candles, I confirm that the last cricket's voice is not the pumpkin's when I still hear, afar, a fragile, fugitive, squeak. Once, however—after November rain had poured through its singed and shrunken top—I found a jack-o-lantern that had filled with water in its base. Yet the tongue that had formed was frozen.

I note the windy Halloweens when I must use my hand to form a protective cup around the match that will light the fire that does not compel the pumpkin to speak. I would hold the match within the red glow of my closed fingers and make a fist-o'-lantern if I could, but I have not the strength of martyrs. As well, a candle ignited before insertion into the pumpkin has slim chance of staying lighted on its own. But once the universal candlelight is shielded by the rind, a grand, Personal, orange, glow starts to outshine the meek universalities! A stable star begins to form!

Before I move to the back of the jack-o'-lantern's head to study the pure glow of the lighted rind, I take one last look at the front. Through the carved face I confirm only the color of the candle and of its white light. I see this meek white light through the shapes I have imposed on the face: often mostly triangles, like the spaces formed inside of a man's arms held akimbo in pride. When I linger before a jack-o'-lantern's front I marvel that the same faces appear by the same hands each year, but also that those same faces appear, too, by different hands of different families—just as all families, at last, seem to have the same photographs. One day it will be conceded it was not *Jones* nor *Smith* nor, say, some future wave of *Rodriguez* that held prominence in the American census. Nay, it was and is the *O'Lanterns* - the true, silent majority. In order to suggest this tribal breadth, I have noted that citizens have started to use jack-o'-lanterns like a canvas for broad scenes rather than as a marble for rendering an individualized face, and on those canvases are vast, Pangea-sized representations on the little globular pumpkin. But whether one carves a personalized, singular face or whether one renders a gaping, collective, vastness on the front of a pumpkin, only varying degrees of the meek, white, universal light of the candle are exposed through the holes.

I leave the face, and I go to the back of my lighted jack-o'-lantern, to its blank, Pacific side, to the purest source of the glowing, Personal, orange light on the uncarved hemisphere of the rind. There I see, at last, what I see, as well, from the back of my beloved's head. There my beloved most resembles no one. There I recognize her still, but there she shows no weakness, as would her face, from influence. There she is most she for she cannot react to me, and I cannot react to her.

The jack-o'-lantern, too: he can't be made to speak this paradoxical power of a globular summary that yet suggests the supremacy of the Individual. It can only be witnessed on the back of his head.

Looking for Polly Benedict

I find myself single again after decades of freedom from the cares of courtship and dating. Though I am a man in his fifties, I find myself often taking walks in my native village of Northport, New York, and there I review the childhood impressions that confirmed my conduct in the romantic treatment of women. I walk down a hill from the home in which I spent my boyhood and make my way to Main Street, and from there I climb to the summit of a steep hill and pay my respects in the evening light to my elementary school. It was there that the foundation of my romantic code was first submitted to me. Ocean Avenue School stands high above all the buildings below on Main Street, higher than even the church steeples, and thus my childish heart perceived my school to be a sort of Yankee temple. It is an imposing, red brick structure, that suggested to me, even then, the civil religious grandeur that WPA lodges of the National Park System command in the wilderness. The flagpole of Ocean Avenue School, which presided then over a painted map of the United States on the pavement of the courtyard, seemed to me it must be the periscope of God, raised from a secret vessel commanded by the Lord, he dressed after the style of Admiral Farragut or Uncle Sam. When a few children from St. Philip's elementary school climbed the hill each week to rehearse with our orchestra, they wearing then their distressed and untucked uniforms (stained with afternoons), I had the impression that they must be the poor children of the village.

In the central lobby of Ocean Avenue School at Christmastime was a large Christmas tree; but its magic was secondary to a vision I witnessed just a few feet beyond it one evening, while standing in a doorway that entered the auditorium. After finishing my turn with the younger children at the Christmas concert, I watched with awe as the chorus of the older grades formed a living Christmas tree—by holding lanterns covered with red and green theater gels—as they sat and swayed on the risers. The words of Meredith Wilson's "It's Beginning to Look a Lot Like Christmas" advised me in a very particular way: "Take a look in the Five and Ten, glistening once again, with candy canes and silver lanes aglow." I also noted: "There's a tree in the grand hotel, one in the park as well, the sturdy kind that doesn't mind the snow."

Because the Main Street that thrived in the village below answered with such strict and concrete parallels to the lyrical details of this song, soon no walk home from school ever seemed without a strict correspondence between the lyrical and the actual, between an earnest Americana of ideas and an earnest Americana of the senses.

Northport and its Main Street comprised a village of no national significance preserved as if it had such a significance, perhaps because it stood as an emblem of an idealized, beautiful, average— an average raised to a zenith by its persistence: churches, old movie house, village hall, fire house, Five and Ten, sweet shop, small grocery, candy store—all surrounding a Main Street never forced to dwindle, but to dead-end in its apotheosis by a perpendicular meeting with the harbor, with the start of the abstraction of the sea.

Ocean Avenue School led us on many fieldtrips on foot to Main Street, and the romance that infused those missions was achieved by the stupendous implications of a fundamental choreography: we walked in pairs, girls on the inside, boys on the outside. Thus, on the voyage out, I saw always to my right the instability and dangers of traffic; on my left, on the inside—as if a supporting part of the architecture of churches, movie house, village hall, fire house, five and ten, sweet shop, small grocery store, candy store—I always saw a little girl. I think now of one grand field trip: when the entire school walked down the hill (boys on the outside, girls on the inside) to see *The Muppet Movie*.

This film was no mere production for children, but, instead, it reflected the moral sensibilities that had prevailed when Hollywood still enforced a Production Code for itself—a code that had coasted from a Judeo-Christian pattern and yet served to make that pattern for America at the same time (forming a sort of perpetual motion machine of morality); the market honed the wares, and the wares honed the market. The Production Code had been grand for it had represented a self-censorship that had to meet the demands of a disciplined people. A code that itself had coasted out of the greatest gold currencies of civilization then coasted into the paper currencies of its own successors, for even after the Code was abolished from Hollywood, its essence still had a latent momentum as that of a message in a bottle carried into a resistless vacuum, detectable in some of the strongest movies from the decade of my childhood.

The essence of *The Muppet Movie* and "It's Beginning to Look a Lot Like Christmas" began to join hands like golden brothers in my mind. *The Muppet Movie* seemed to coast by a push from the same temperament and impulse of culture that had created a song like "It's Beginning to Look a Lot Like Christmas"—even if the latter had not been written for a movie. By these associations I was getting closer to a faith that a further examination of Main Street's actualities would complete.

But first I was still enthralled by the importation of the entire school body into the movie theater that afternoon. The population of an entire civil religious temple has been marched into another. The little girl I had shielded on the journey was still on my left. But in the seat behind me sat one of my male classmates, Devin. During an early instance from the movie's cameos, Devin leaned forward and impressed me with a whisper that seemed very mature: "That's James Coburn!"

Devin had seen the movie already during an evening performance. I thus thought of a film that

I, as well, had seen there after school hours and in the company of my mother and father: *Superman: The Movie*—another creation that seemed to coast from the power of an earlier time. The film's first spoken line is from a little boy in the role of narrator, he thus sitting on the same side of the cinematic fourth wall as myself: "In the decade of the 1930s. . . ." And as I sat next to my female classmate during *The Muppet Movie*, I recalled a reaction given in *Superman: The Movie* by the villain's glamorous moll, Miss Tessmacher, to a newspaper column: "It's too good to be true. He's 6'-4", has black hair, blue eyes, doesn't drink, doesn't smoke, and tells the truth!" The latter part of Miss Tessmacher's challenge—noting the things Superman *does not* do—struck me as a longing for traits of a lapsed code, what a woman would have from all men if recoverable. Save for the physical description of Superman, there was not one thing on the list that I thought beyond the powers of even a small boy of Earth to resurrect. I listened to Miss Tessmacher with great care, my silence enforced by the binding force of red Swedish Fish adhering between my upper and lower teeth.

After *The Muppet Movie* ended that afternoon, we marched back to school, and once more I was positioned between the dangers of traffic on one side and the intricate suggestiveness of a little girl and the facades of Main Street on the other. Kermit's final words were in my mind, "Life's like a movie, write your own ending," and thus the incarnation of my romantic resolutions was nearly complete.

The completion would come with the arrival of another Christmas. Between the movie theater and the Five and Ten was the firehouse. There was I taken to see Santa Claus, and as one waited on the line that stretched out to Main Street, I heard, now playing from the public address system of the firehouse—so that the gaps between the growing number of temples seemed almost obliterated now—"Take a look in the Five and Ten, glistening once again, with candy canes and silver lanes aglow." In this instance the voice was Bing Crosby's, but just as imperative as the words seemed still this second time was the alchemy of the monaural hiss and crackle of the recording's silent but noisy intro wax, suggesting that a preceding age's temperament can impose its influence on the vacuum of the present.

Thus I went straight to the outside of the Five and Ten after visiting with Saint Nick. I took a look, through the windows, into the Five and Ten as I had been instructed, and then my civil religious instruction was complete, for there, glistening, was exact Correspondence; for there were candy canes and silver lanes aglow. Meredith Wilson, the songwriter, had ascended from Tin Pan Alley bard to prophet.

And then my mind argued further: If the song was linked to the time of the Production Code, and thereby *to* a code, then the song's indisputable correspondence to Main Street's concrete materiality (both its inside and its outside) linked indissolubly the actualities of Main Street to moral certainties. Main Street had become the scene of a Revelation for my civil religion. The very structure of Actuality had become the Code, a code, to me. And if by the Code I had to shield a little girl in front of the Five and Ten from the traffic at my back as I beheld the silver lanes within, and since I had thereby linked the idea of Woman with the very facades of Main Street, she became as the vestibule of Main Street's complete Correspondence, and thus of its inner world and as the sexual guardian of my future world; for a man of the Code must be worthy of all things he would enter.

With these ideas now in place, I permitted myself to enter the Five and Ten. The inside of Mr. Winderoff's store was as much a match as the outside to the prophecy, and as if to compound a young boy's introduction to such a dense Correspondence, twin sisters—the Johnson twins—presided over their own respective registers on opposite sides of the first floor, suggesting a balance as that which must rule over an angel's wings.

As that year's Christmas continued to near, in the early fading light that enwrapped my walks home along Main Street, I finished the final proof of the great Correspondence. For the song said, too, "There's a tree in the grand hotel, one in the park as well, the sturdy kind that doesn't mind the snow."

There indeed was the tall and sturdy tree in the Village Park. The hotel that had stood nearby had been razed before my lifetime, but I met this challenge of reconciliation in noting that Northport's World War II monument now occupied that site; memorials of the Code's time and realizations of the Code were interchangeable to me. And yet the tree from that grand hotel still seemed to stand, for a tree was erected each year at the very base of Main Street, right on the edge of the harbor, seemingly moved from the vanished lobby that had stood only yards away.

As if my new religion required that I contribute to the vitality of the Correspondence I had discovered—that I become an agent of the more subtle and fluid junctions between symbols of the Code and its civic actualities—it became my duty to find the spot each year where the flashing traffic light at Main's final intersection could be made to seem the tree's star from the observer's point of view. Sometimes this effect is realized by standing almost at the point of that final intersection: Main, Woodbine, and Bayview. In other years I have not been able to achieve this result until I am as far back as #76 Main. Other years I can only become the civil religious lamplighter by standing somewhere in between these two marks. I walk until the light aligns; I affect to recreate and evangelize the premonitory swaying of the older children of the chorus who had held colored lamps whilst singing Mr. Wilson's gospel.

This Correspondence reigned still in my heart and mind even when, as I have observed, I was compelled to return to my native Main Street once more in my middle age, then as single again as if I were still a boy at Ocean Avenue School. I permitted a cold keyboard and an algorithm to match me with a beautiful, younger woman, a photographer. We had coffee meetings in her neighborhood, and then we spent an afternoon exploring the derelict buildings of the condemned Kings Park Psychiatric hospital, an adventure she described as a "photographer's dream." We returned to my home above Main Street so that we could change for dinner. When she emerged, I was in awe of her beauty. Her long black hair and exquisite prettiness were complemented by a black denim skirt, black stockings and black shoes, and a blouse with a muted leopard pattern in small print. All this framed a flawless, stone-cold, vulpine figure. If the movie camera is said to add ten pounds, then one suspects that movie goddesses must appear excessively thin in person. Maintained by the outline of this woman before me, however, was a soft, thin, seductive layer that a cinematic camera could thus only betray. She was designed as a perfection for the camera of man's eye, the camera that adds nothing but only receives.

I was thrilled to have this woman on my arm as we went down the hill toward the street that approached Main. I relished that our sides were pressed hard against the other's because it was a cold night, yet when we reached the first sidewalk I made an effort to be on the outside. Somehow in the unrehearsed choreography of that moment I caused her to lose an earring that we soon had to give up as lost in the darkness and the old snow. But we continued to the intersection that would reveal Main after a hard right turn, just under the flash of the traffic light. In the blackness of the winter night Main Street's outline appeared unchanged, yet I began suddenly to meditate alterations that had occurred since boyhood but had given me no pause until that moment.

All the buildings and their faces remained, but nearly all the businesses of the past had vanished. I could not take a look in the Five and Ten, for it was gone. Main Street appeared like a Yankee's Mesa Verde to me.

I paused for an instant before entering the restaurant we had selected for dinner. At this location on

Main Street in the past had been the little *A & J* grocery store. One afternoon, when I had been a boy in my golden age of Correspondence, I stood before the *A & J* and waited for my mother, who was shopping nearby. A very old woman approached me (I realize now that she must have been born in the nineteenth-century), and she had a five-dollar bill in her fingers. She extended the bill toward me with a shaking and brittle hand.

"Can you buy me a pound of onions?" she asked. My sense of Correspondence had grown so rich that I replied sincerely, "I don't know how." I thought her request would involve a complex challenge of taking measurements in respect to a scale and a complicated bout of arithmetic to establish the right change, and I would not dare to enter the store if I could not perform the task. The woman looked irritated. She did not go in the store herself, and she moved on down the sidewalk. Not long ago, I saw a homeless woman in New York's Penn Station. Her face somehow reminded me of the old lady who had asked that I buy her onions nearly fifty years ago. When the homeless woman approached me, I put aside my usual caution in such cases and bought her food.

Standing before the old building of the *A & J* with my date but seeing instead a fancy restaurant behind the grocery store's familiar facade made me uneasy. I resolved, however, that if Main Street no longer provided a strict Correspondence, I would treat it as a backlot. Had not the art of the Code required such sleight of hand? I might find the wrong interior, the wrong soundstage for the *A & J* behind its once Corresponding facade, but I could still play the role of an honorable Correspondence whilst dining with my glamorous date. The corresponding soundstage for the *A & J* would be I myself.

"I know how," I whispered, and we went into the restaurant. We were seated side by side at a little round table in an appealing, dark corner. I really liked this girl, and it is difficult for me now to recall when I started to count the number of vodkas she had consumed. I was still trying to prove to Miss Tessmacher that my resolutions were not too good to be true, even though for most women this leads to the suspicion I am merely a recovering alcoholic. However, my abstinence seemed of little note at this dinner. Though I held to my religion, soon I must have looked like a Guy Kibbee character dining with a woozy chorus girl from a pre-Code film. I felt embarrassed yet flattered as she pulled me close by draping her legs over mine and then squeezing my cheeks before giving long kisses. It made me nervous that a family with young children was at a table nearby.

When dinner was over I settled the check and guided my unsteady date to the street. "I - want - *spawinkles!*" she exclaimed with a slur, by which she meant the sprinkles that one puts on top of ice cream. We had bought ice cream earlier in the day for dessert at home after dinner. "He'll give us some spawinkles!" she said, and the young woman pointed at a lone teenager in a window, he standing mournfully behind the counter of an empty ice cream parlor nearing its closing time.

"I don't think he can just give us sprinkles," I replied as she began to tack along the sidewalk back to my home. Her course was so deviating and unsteady that I could not hold to a dedicated position on the outside. I was not protecting her from traffic but from herself (always to a degree insulting to one who retains a fraction of sobriety and chooses to see the protection as condescension).

We returned to my home. The Code of Correspondence compels one to be more sexually charged than even the most reckless sensualist, for it commands one to sense that the greatest intensity can only be earned by an elaborate ceremoniousness. Thus, at the end of the evening, she lay prone at my side, but prematurely submitting before ceremony was satisfied. She was safe in her submission for common safety's sake, for she was correct that I presented no threat. However, she did not sense my disappointment in suspecting that she did not comprehend the vision that drove my will to present further proof. She could not intuit the subtlety of my disappointment. She lay baffled at my side, and I lay at her side, offering a protection that she did not desire. In her innocent modernity, she twisted a moment of power into an affected impotency, and she forced me to use a discipline that to her suggested only a powerless moment. She said more than once as we only embraced, "You're so polite." I looked at her leopard print blouse, hanging on the back of a chair. For a moment I thought of it as if only a trophy of my own skin, and of how it is said that many big cats, even if hungry, refrain from delivering a coup de grace unless the precise order of their hunting steps is observed.

This beautiful young woman had herself

intensified the present backlot shambles of Main Street and that restaurant. She was a backlot herself. Thus, though familiar and gorgeous still on the outside, she was nothing I could enter. Instead, I lay on the outer edge of the bed, between her and the windows looking out to the traffic of the road, and I tried to rebuild Main Street in my mind; and when I checked on her after she fell asleep, I tried to imagine her pretty face as if restored to the top of a sturdily controlled body, as I had done when aligning the traffic light with the top of the Christmas tree at the harbor's edge.

Walking on the outside of the sidewalk in childhood had confirmed for me the vastness of a Correspondence into which Woman was soldered not as a symbol but as a comprehensive Cosmos, matching inside and outside as had the vanished Main Street. Thus: even at her most glamourous—nay, paradoxically, most so then—Woman had never been an object, but a glistening world, in which I was but a citizen. Thus: Betty Grable painted on the nose of a spitfire: that was no mere pornography but a depiction of man's deepest mortally- and spiritually-protective affect, placing the pilot between her and the traffic of doom.

Yet all this is only the thought of a solitary man on the edge of bed with a relative stranger in the silver lanes of moonlight. Somehow, I wanted to see her again, and wondered if I had made some headway with her by my actions. But that impulse is like that of presenting a purchased ticket to an indifferent usher in a theater with a dwindling house after intermission, or to a sleeping conductor in an empty midnight coach. I save it in the latter case, but I am rarely given an invitation that will give me cause to use the unpunched ticket on another train.

Trapestry

At first I thought the story had everything to do with the piano. As a young undergraduate, the piano had augmented my already considerable sense of self-confidence, yet in striving to make myself inaccessible to all women but the imagined and idealized future *one*, a strange caution set in when a likely *one* appeared and herself seemed inaccessible and unobtainable. But in the latter half of her final semester, in the autumn of 1991, the young violinist—tall, porcelain, irresistibly vital and convivial; with a mane of hair as curled and complex as a thousand bundled, undeployed violin strings; with a beauty of face not so much like any one famous actress but suggestive of many in their heyday, and thus distinctive in a kaleidoscopic patent—suggested we read chamber works together. Many a duet pairing, though well-matched musically, may also start for the same ulterior reasons that inspire many other kinds of superficially strict professional alliances. That possibility made me accept the invitation immediately; under all other circumstances I would have remained content to exult in the piano's regal, solitary completeness—a singleness that can even find satisfaction in dividing one's self into further solitary fractions by practicing hands separately. I contained my romantic hopes at the start, but soon I cultivated them as the young woman and I spent more time together after our readings, even though she would depart for graduate school in England in the New Year.

This romance on Long Island—as elevated and innocent in my memory as a Hays Code Dream, a dream fit for the Motion Picture Production Code established in 1934—unfolded in the last two months of the year—months, here in the American northeast, that have always stood for a mounting sense of imminence for me, which are marked by the final thinning of the cricket choir into isolated soloists, the passing of the last signs of Halloween, the further darkening and cooling that frames Thanksgiving, and the final but artificial flash of Christmas light that concludes in leafless dark and cold. The growing absence of scent that comes with the mounting cold that burns the inner nose has always encouraged me to perceive, in relief against the surrendering outer vitality of the year, a personal inner life that seems to stand alone, unvanquished, constant, eternally cheerful notwithstanding the increasing and, at last, complete absence of external reinforcement. The apotheosis of these months tests and confirms the Idealist—he who is certain that what comes from within always trumps what comes from without. I have long suspected that the early Church had more than conquest and convenience in mind when it placed Christ's birthday near to the dates of established Pagan rites in late December. The mutual though perhaps unwitting recognition of the suggestiveness of cold's victory over scent may have caused *all* parties to contend for the same dates on the calendar. In the air of December that burns away the scent of all that is without, I become as a self-church, one that finds a sort of solitary Easter within during such dark and thrilling and scentless evenings.

But on a glorious night in December of 1991 in Huntington Village, walking from the movie theater to Swensen's Ice Cream Parlor on Main Street, I could smell her perfume though my nose burned with cold. My fierce Idealism was thus confronted with the core of a kindlier churchly philosophy—that another may be as conscious as myself—this by the irreligious and outrageous vitality of her young body, laughing and standing against the cold. Her body was even more than this to me. Notwithstanding the scentless and icy air, the young woman seemed the sole and concentrated preserve of all the force and vitality of the past- and distant-future-living parts of the cyclic year. In that hale December bitterness, as the autumn gasped and yielded to new winter, the white and slender columns of her legs seemed a raw memorial of the surrendered spring and summer. No, the monument was more living to me than what it signified. The deadness of the cold air amplified her bodily beauty. To see a young woman's legs in winter—as I would later see them that month, too, in a short, red velvet Christmas party dress—especially as she may dash from car to indoors, made my eyes relish more than all things the concentrated demonstration of feminine alabaster that thrived notwithstanding the deathly cold. This sight seen in the moment of such transition is indispensable to understanding a young man's sexual preoccupations that are, at last, completely above the sexual. The shocking sight of her white legs in the leafless blackness was something akin to what one feels in seeing a healthy pumpkin survive into winter. No, for the pumpkin is doomed. But the legs thrive, radiate, bloom even in a hothouse of shattered windows.

If asked, at last, when it was that I encountered the zenith of youth, I would venture that cold night in Huntington in 1991. I hear even now in my mind's ear my laughter, and the girl's, as I struggled with the stick-shift of a red Volkswagon Beetle convertible, as I drove along Sabbath Day Path near the village green at the night's end. I would have to answer Gabriel with something of a riddle, as well: that I had felt most holy when at my most bodily.

The young violinist left for England and graduate school just after the New Year. She said she would write to me, and she did. I ended my reply with an unnecessary valediction—one that contended that I would write no more, for continued correspondence would be as a "tacit pledge of fidelity." I was not seeking other romances, and I still thought the Cosmos of this one, but that phrase seemed best to one who was looking for the noble line by which to realize a Hays Code apotheosis. Yet in the following decades I continued to recall the extraordinarily accomplished and beautiful young woman who, when we sat across from one another at Swensen's, had also blown at me the wrapper of her straw.

My romances then became less guided by the Hays Code and defined better by the disappointments of the B-players in modern romantic comedies. At the end of each of those stories I thought of the cold night along the Sabbath Day Path and checked the internet to see where the violinist might be. I took no action. One night, however, a year after I had regained my freedom yet again, I searched online once more, and I noted the email address of the law firm for which the violinist now worked. I wrote to her; I had an immediate and gracious reply. We had cordial exchanges, and her warmth extended, as well, to an invitation to dinner with her husband and very young daughter in Connecticut. I declined. I let another year pass, and I wrote again to say hello. She invited me again to visit her family in Connecticut, and to try her new piano. I baulked once more. But this second new correspondence then led, weeks later, to our plan to meet at our alma mater for a chamber music reading session. This was for February 6, 2020— almost twenty-nine years since I had last seen her.

As I made my drive to our 11 AM appointment at Queens College in Flushing, I endeavored to picture in my mind an unrecognizable, old woman so that I would not be shocked and so that the day would be passed in pleasant memory no matter whom, in a sense, I would encounter that morning. After an hour's drive, and after a bit of hunting on the streets for parking, I found a spot not far from the campus on a side street. I phoned the violinist to tell her where I had parked, and she told me to go directly to the school and not to wait in the rain. I went into the nearest building. The violinist called and said that she had found a parking place on the same street as I had. I said I would come out to meet her. I held firm to my image of the imagined old lady. Soon I saw her on the other side of the street—a bit to the west, coming from the side street's corner to the crosswalk. I was shocked, for I had to dismiss my image of someone made unrecognizable by time. We waved to each other. She crossed the street, and soon we came together for a hug.

"You look exactly the same!" I exclaimed. She smiled and paid a compliment to my navy blue pea coat.

We talked all the way to the music school and then made our way to a little practice room. We read through many pieces, and many were from the same list from decades earlier. The room was warm—no, hot—and we took more than one break in the hallway, during which I gave her two books that I had written, and she gave me a bottle of maple syrup from her property's trees.

I feared that our day would end with our playing, but she asked if I would like to have lunch. I began to unleash my memories and regrets as we made our way to the side street where we had parked. We found, when we went to her car, that she had been issued a ticket, but I had not. We had a joyful ride to lunch via the Long Island Expressway. On the way I permitted myself to unleash all my memories of the romance from 1991's end—and the reasoning behind my letter in answer to hers from London in the winter of 1992.

As I write these lines, I look down now upon the lunch receipt that I saved and tipped into my journal. With that receipt pressed flush against the tabletop between us, and my fingers upon its two narrow-most edges, I had pushed those ends together slowly, my hands moving in contrary motion, until two normally separated interior points of the paper met and thus caused a parenthetical bow to form above—that upper portion representing to me the intermediary span of time between two distantly spaced meetings, that upper loop appearing then parenthetical (but somehow remaining latently agent in the tally of chronology), yet the two new touching points on the level plane below also seeming sequentially adjacent. The woman understood my meaning (as she seemed to understand all the things I wished to express). Many may describe this feeling as, "It felt as if no time had passed at all." But I am certain there is much more to it—as in a musical rondo one still registers the intermediary sections between the *A* sections, but the *A* sections, when they return, somehow still feel adjacent, unseparated.

On the printed side of this saved receipt, the text (Panera Bread Café #4657, New Hyde Park, New York, 3:13:30 PM) is fading away (as I have noted happens on many old receipts). But on the blank side of the receipt, written in my own hand below the date, is the word *Trapestry*. Underneath that lone word I had bracketed a pair of words, one over the other: *Tragedy* and *Tapestry*. *Trapestry*, by process of etymological conflation and stirrings of the heart, was our coinage for the fleeting gift of the day, expressed by the fragile demonstration I made with that very receipt.

Before the lunch was over the violinist looked at me in misty earnest and said that the day was a once-in-a-lifetime kind of experience. I agreed. We drove back to my car via a network of streets and not by the Expressway. We sat in her car for a time before I returned to mine. The violinist said she was thinking of how we might proceed—and with very tacit expressions invoked all that had to be considered. I replied that I understood, of course, and that it was to her credit that she made such allusions. For many things had not been said that day, and I abetted the omissions by giving in to the very seductive trap of not asking about them. Before I left for my car she said, "I feel like I've been hit by a truck."

The next day, an almost daily correspondence began, and I remarked: "No single man should leave, by his lack of verbal caution, a stunning married woman feeling as if hit by a truck." Yet we began a pattern, of meeting almost every two to three weeks for reading chamber music and having lunch. The meetings always observed the demonstrable forms of friendship, yet I always had to govern the unusable impulses that boiled within me as a free man. At one of our lunches, as we recalled our time at the ice cream parlor from three decades earlier, she pursed her lips and then blew the wrapper of her straw at me again. I would remind myself: "She has more to lose; I have more not to gain."

I would wait with excitement for her as she walked off of the Cross-Sound Ferry and arrived in Port Jefferson for the start of our days together, and I would sometimes notice the papery bodies of horseshoe crabs on the nearby beach, suggesting Normandy casualties to me. But the ease of her arrivals by ferry made it seem as if the loop that hovered over the Trapestry receipt had no figurative part of her crossings across the water from Connecticut.

On cool days she would walk toward me wearing a wrap and sporting lithe boots, yet wearing jeans that covered her still slender legs—looking like a photo of equestrian briskness from a Laura Ashley catalog—and she seemed to carry only printed scores, and her violin case slung across her back like a quiver.

When nearly a year of this pattern had unfolded and the air grew cold once more, I told the violinist as she walked from the ferry with me to my car that the underlying absence of scent from the frigid air had recalled to me the memory of decades earlier of the one scent that had thrived in such a void. As we climbed into my car she smiled and recalled the dramatic name of the perfume she had worn when we were in college. Then she added that her daughter told her that she always smells like sugar cookies.

She revealed to me that she still had the letter I had sent to her in London in early 1992. I was shocked to see it again, and I pretended to laugh with her at my subscription at the letter's end, written in affectation of the closing of a page from a Samuel Richardson epistolary novel. But my attention was focused, however, on the phrase not far above my signature—and there it was, still, the line about continued correspondence seeming to me a tacit pledge of fidelity.

The violinist said she had looked again at my letter around 2008, and that at one time, as well, she had found a photo of me on the internet, posed with other musicians. "Did they look like a group of singers?" I asked. No, it had been musicians, she replied, and then we both laughed at the easy reflex it is for an instrumentalist to refrain from calling a singer a musician. She expressed embarrassment for her remark. But I assured this accomplished and beautiful woman that she was no snob, that she had raised the standard so high that if one is going to have romantic regrets about lost love, then one should place them on the highest object.

She ventured to me that "there seemed to be no wagons in my house," after our readings overlapped more than one time with my family: my mother, father, and sister. She said she felt she was at times, when back in her own home, as a cat pulling a wagon behind her—that she was in traces that should be occupied by a team of draft horses. I assured her that all families have their covered wagons. I could see that she had the burden of one-in-a-census energy, vitality, and joy, this woman who surprised me with quotations that she revealed were from my own books, and who lobbied for me as a pianist with the rarest kind of attentive agency.

She wondered aloud if I should have gone with her to England. Then she suggested that though we were not together as we may have wanted, that we had each other now after a different fashion. I thanked her for the astonishing way that she sees things. I speculated that perhaps the outcome was optimal, a higher realization than had we pursued a young love in 1991.

I texted her after she left that day: "Thank you so much, all-vital but harness-bound but inimitable and glorious Wagon Cat! The world would not move but for the enfired pulling of the likes of you! There is, however, no like, I should say—no like of or to the singular. Pull on! Pull on!"

We continued to meet, write, and exchange phone calls. I could hear that she was crying on one day when I reached her by phone. Her husband had asked her to end our friendship. I told her that she could tell him for me that ever since I was a child and had first seen the movie *Camelot*, I had hated Lancelot's guts, and thus his wife was safe in this knight's care. This helped for a time, but even I realized that in professing my contempt for Lancelot I was thus confessing to a sort of self-hatred.

I took a run at this time with a trusted friend along the shoreline of Long Island Sound, and Connecticut looked close and clear in the cold winter light. I had introduced the violinist to my friend sometime before, and now on the privacy of the beach I spoke of my dilemma. My friend is an observant fellow and a self-confessed former "dirty-dog." We paused at our turn-around point of the run. "She has got it *all!*" he began, as a man might exclaim after he conjures an ideal woman in the holodeck of Picard's U.S.S. *Enterprise*. Then came the wry addition: "Including a husband!"

After the grim humor had passed, he asked: "You do know this has nothing to do with the violin?" The wisdom of a reformed rake always carries a special power of invulnerability to the Puritan who frets over his ostensibly perfect record.

During all this time I continued to practice the piano. I was working on the finale of Bach's G-Major Toccata. I was rehearsing it hands separately. But it occurred to me—because inner lines pass from one hand to the other in relay when such pieces are performed—that by working this way I was creating the impression that artificial cul-de-sacs blocked the open boulevards that run between the two hands when they work in normal complement—those two hands conducting a relay so subtle, facile, and seamless that any observer on the figurative bleachers would contend that they had witnessed nothing but an unsupported, floating baton traveling in runnerless lanes.

What cannot be heard by an outside witness but as a single unbroken line, is known to the pianist to be the union of two parts of a divided self giving a singular impression. The practical choreography of a pianist is an expression of intolerance for the sins of omission. I resumed practicing with two hands and thought of the Trapestry receipt—then went to my laptop so as to write a message that would win me the race to the high ground, to the genuine apotheosis, at last, of a Hays Code dream.

But there I found an email from the violinist saying that we should end our alliance. She said, in essence, that our continued correspondence would be as a pledge of tacit fidelity. I realized that she had not been making easy ferry rides, but undertaking a hard portage of her own, as when a kayaker notices that a secret dram of the separated waters is always carried overland in the cockpit. She had been wrestling in her own way with an overarching bow of Trapestry, perhaps reinforced by her own solitary practicing, in which case it had everything to do with the violin.

The Myth of Absolute Unison

In my student days, after long hours of working at the piano, I would take to the sidewalks of my native village for respite. The enforced solitude of practicing perhaps infected me with a bit of youthful bitterness, leaving me with prejudice as I engaged in my study of sidewalk etiquette. Couples in the thrall of romance, who walk hand-in-hand—and who approach one from the opposite direction on a sidewalk—make the same demand, very often, as that of a single person of considerable width: that they are unwilling to accommodate opposing traffic. Thus many who are desperate to leave their single state so as to be in a romantic pairing have the dream that the romance will render them, to a degree, still with an indissoluble singleness.

A couple reaches for the Myth of Unison when they clasp hands. When that pair endeavors, at last, to eradicate all distinguishing space between them, and in the rapture of intercourse a man attempts to occupy the same space as his woman by penetration, alas! nine months later the common result is still another individual. Permit me to draw a distinction between the aim of handholding by lovers and that by those who concede the impossibility of the Myth of Unison: the uneasy truces during familial professions of grace, the protective guidance offered to children, and the linking of actors' hands on stage, hiding chains of enmities during a curtain call. But few lovers enter their stories without a nearly comprehensive faith in the possibility of Absolute Unison: belief in the dream that there can be an intensification of a singular utterance from two separate sources that yet occupy somehow *distinguishably* the exact same location. It is hard, at times, to understand this faith in Unison, a faith, again, best embodied by clasped hands across sidewalks, when even by other touches between lovers' hands a benign hint of disillusion can be spotted—as when, say, during moments of romantic assurance or consolation across a table, one hand must land atop the other, and thus there is a hint of hierarchy. In romantic comedies, Fate is often suggested when two strangers reach for the same object. But the reach is the limit of the shared experience; one hand or another must prevail if possession of the object it to follow.

But romantic couples deserve pardon for their faith, for even the principal forces in Western music, keyboard instruments, have developed as if with the dream of Absolute Unison as their ultimate aim. What is an Absolute Unison in music? Its practical predecessor from actuality is the common unison: this kind of unison executed on an instrument other than the piano necessitates distance between the points of utterance—whether the mere distance of less than an inch between two strings on, say, a violin, or the greater distance between two separate instruments (sounded by two locations on one instrument in the former case, or by two locations from two different instruments in the latter). Such common unisons are, at last, in the ultimate physical and thus comprehensive sense, only ostensible. But keyboard instruments, particularly the piano, endeavor to realize the idea of Absolute Unison, the dream of the most ardent lovers - endeavoring to eliminate the material distance between points of identical utterance, so that those sources of identical utterance occupy the exact same point of physical origin—and, further still, even reach to make component parts of a single performing self realize an Absolute Unison.

But, alas, as for lovers, this is a dream. The message revealing the Myth of Absolute Unison, unlike the meanings some hope to find in vinyl records played backward, is hidden in plain sight, best decoded in moments of both playing and hearing some of the keyboard's greatest masterworks, especially of the eighteenth-century.

As vocal music yielded in supremacy to keyboard music in Western history, the latter did not fail to borrow the former's polyphonic tendency to have separate voices at times overlap and cross (like tracks in a railyard)—and the transient result of such collisions would be unisons: two voices uttering the same pitch in the same register at the same time. Much of the keyboard music in the eighteenth-century and earlier that relished frequent invocation of unison was conceived for instruments with two manuals (two keyboards), rendering a measurable distance between the two points of identical utterance and distance between the two hands engaged in the choreography of execution. J. S. Bach's "Goldberg" Variations of 1741 has countless instances of such overlapping railyards of unison, but the hands are prevented from colliding because each hand is placed, in many sections of the piece, on its own respective keyboard.

For the sake of analogy to the above, imagine looking down from the sky, directly above a two-story apartment building made entirely of glass. The layouts of the apartments on both floors are exactly the same, even unto placement of furnishings and appliances. A man lives in one apartment; a woman lives in the other. They have taken a romantic interest in each other, and both are observed (from above) moving to the same spot in their respective apartments in order to share their first phone call. Both are nearly the same size as people, and both have equally dark hair. As they move into place for the call, to the observer above the couple appears to merge as if into one figure. From above they appear to occupy the exact same space in the Cosmos. They do not appear to collide, and the common unison of their budding love appears to originate from a shared point in space. One does not appear to yield to the other as they use phones and chairs that appear as if on the same spot on the same plane. But should the couple's romance progress, and they move in together, the original illusory observation from above can no longer be made—for then, even while still looking down through the glass roof, we know that the couple has moved from a common unison to the collisions inherent in reaching for the dream of Absolute Unison. The two lovers can never command the exact same position at the exact same time. They are reminded that a common unison in sound and spirit requires space between the sources of utterance; a common unison requires an interval!

A keyboard player who observes his hands approaching the choreography of a common unison in many of the two-manual variations of Bach's "Goldberg" Variations witnesses something very much akin to the glimpse one may have of the lovers' first telephone conversation sketched above. But Music seems to harbor the same dream as our lovers. During Bach's time, a composer wrote keyboard music with no certainty of which type of keyboard a player may possess (organ, clavichord, harpsichord, early pianoforte); thus even works conceived principally for two-manuals (like the "Goldberg Variations") were written to admit the choreographic efforts of the player who may only possess an instrument with one manual.

A pianist who observes his hands approaching the choreography of a common unison in many of the two-manual variations of Bach's "Goldberg" Variations witnesses something very much akin to the choreography of collision in which the lovers engage after they have begun cohabitation, after they have begun their valiant reach for the dream of Absolute Unison. The pianist tracks his own two hands coming together, just as the now cohabitating lovers may attempt to stand in one, precise, shared location. Yet the sharing can only be approximated; only one hand can have supreme influence on the aural attack of the nominally shared key, just as one person in the cohabitating couple must be dominant for a fleeting and strident instant when any attempt is made for a reach toward a precise and mutual occupation of coordinates. Only one can have principal occupancy and effect on a precise location. One can detect such moments of the reach for Absolute Unison while listening to or practicing the "Goldberg" Variations' double-manual sections at a piano (when the two hands contend for strict mutual space like clasped hands fighting to engage in supremacy for an emergency chest compression), just as in the throes of early and earnest romance; one senses such moments in both cases as a jolt from the sudden absence of the power of two. There is a jolt from the power of obligated omission—because though the dream of Absolute Unison calls for the power of two to emerge from a single source, the single source only permits the presiding activator or hand to be heard.

Imagine a two-lane highway made into but one lane without removing the oppositional traffic—the effect is very much akin to taking a piece conceived for two manuals to a piano. (In both cases—highways and piano keyboards—they remain too busy to permit the building of memorials on the precise sites of collisions. Perhaps that is why one sees flowers left often on roadsides and flowers left at the edge of concert hall stages. Frequently a man will give a woman flowers before a romantic collision, but she must put them to the side if she intends to walk with clasped hands. If the dream of Absolute Unison could be realized, would there be any call for flowers?)

I remember that in my early college years as a pianist, I was advised to treat an approaching unison and collision of my two hands upon the piano's single manual as if both distinct musical lines could still be represented in the final landing on the shared key. Yet the lesson from the music was higher than the lesson from the lesson: Only one hand can win, even in the mind's ear! Separate utterance through the same key is impossible; no unison can be realized by two sources occupying the same location. The Absolute Unison is always a dream! The piano, at last, is the supreme teacher of this benign disillusion: that though common unisons, duplications produced from separated sources (as on the two manuals of a double-manual harpsichord) are possible, the single manual of the piano both demands yet proves the impossibility of Absolute Unison—the impossibility of duplications contained within a single source in a single instance of time. Bring one's two hands over a single key and one hand will always prevail in characterizing the utterance. Some kind of concentricity is always at hand; some aspect of a benignly disbalanced complementariness always presides even within the solitary soul. Only one articulation can win. Even the component parts of an individual must yield to the supreme part of the individual's composite makeup. No solitary action is ever augmented by collective action, not even collective action emanating from the solitary self. The leap from common unisons on a double-manual harpsichord to the reach for Absolute Unisons on the single manual of the piano provide the ultimate lesson of the supremacy of the individual. There are no soulmates. There are no unisons, at last—only singular utterances.

Playing a unison on a double-manual harpsichord is like praying with one's hands spread apart, and yet playing a unison on the single manual of a piano, like realizing the truly flushed posture of prayer, only affects the appearance of a unity. Hands are always distinct, as are the component parts of ourselves. "How many angels can dance on the head of a pin?" After confronting the inspiring disillusion taught at the piano by the Myth of Absolute Unison, one submits: "Only one."

Yet a man and a woman in the thrall of seeing each other as two angels will resist the disillusion with a vigorous but at last exhausting alternative, engaging in a dance of alternating leaps to the head of their ardor's pin. As Ira Gershwin suggests, this is nice work if you can get it. And his brother's music, in the finale of his piano concerto, illustrates one who *tries* to get it, by quick alternations of the two hands on one and the same key for the course of an entire movement, an attempt at Absolute Unison by quick and alternating occupations of a mutual space—this, again, like the two lovers, bent on sharing the pedestal upon which they both place the other, hoping to approximate Absolute Unison by trading in rapid successions of box jumps. But alas! In the midst of the frantic approximation of Absolute Unison (by the alternating repetitions of Mr. Gershwin in his concerto's solo part), an orchestra descends (interleaved, rondo-style) as an art-deco hand of God, and even whilst it recognizes and exults in the disillusion it teaches, keeps driving the dream onward—as does some accompaniment to the lovers' dance upon the shared pedestal.

Yet saying all that I do above, I resist the benign disillusion, as do the two lovers—even all these years later after my student days. Standing at the edge of Long Island Sound, looming over my native village like four great fingers, are the red-ringed smokestacks built for the Long Island Lighting Company. One imagines the length of the island to be the great thumb of the colossal hand suggested by the four seething stacks. Across the Sound, on the Connecticut (and Westchester, New York) side of the water, stand similar smokestacks. One imagines these complementary giant fingers, facing each other across the Sound, as hands held up in a comparison of span on a first date—a young lady, say, holding up her hand to measure it against that of her suitor, he a pianist. Yet the intervening water of the Sound prevents the smokestacks from ever pressing flush their figurative palms.

Fate continues to demand—or it happens by some unconscious arrangement of my own—that many of my romances have been with women on the other side of the Sound. I often take the ferry to reach them, and I look up to the near stacks as the vessel pulls away from Long Island, and then I pass the time of the crossing watching the other shoreline's imagined fingers as they appear to reach toward me and Absolute Unison. Yet when they grow near, I look back and see that the fingers of Long Island have pulled away. The water of the Sound, a bridging element, is also a gulf, like the sweat of nervous palms during a first date's clasp.

The perspiration of nerves do the same for the two hands of the pianist as they collide over the same key. I am an individual, then, even against myself. I cannot double myself, create an Absolute Unison from components of my unequal parts or augment my principal utterance with two forces of myself from one location. Every tone, every utterance, is always singular. Bach left a staggering lesson in his hidden message.

Even God forbids Absolute Unison so as to grant us sovereign identity. Though he is immovable, he steps back and admits the sea of a Holy Ghost, even as one's efforts bring one's temples flush to his brow—even if one is a conjoined twin in the mind of the Lord. God enforces a gap where there is no chasm. He never denies the solitary completeness of any individual in Creation. It would seem at first that a man is infinite because he carries the Universe within, but he may in fact be complete because he is barred always so exquisitely from ever conjoining with it.

But, again, notwithstanding all I write, I find myself disembarking and making my way to my dates, even in middle age, driven on by a hope that defies benign disillusion. Thus, one cool night, not long ago in an autumn, I walked with a besieged but lovely single mother on the edge of the north side of the Sound. We walked between the water and the edge of a silent amusement park. How many more cries of desperate, affected, glee one hears from an empty roller coaster during its September hiatus than on any summer night! The screams seem thrown from the still, white, wooden skeleton of the ride and held in the silver grass of Rye, rendered there into miniature by crickets.

There were few others on the boardwalk that night, and though we did not clasp hands, we walked arm-in-arm, affecting a pianist's crossing of hands, a crossing that immediately reaches beyond and forsakes the two-handed grasp towards Absolute Unison—like a hope that persists after disillusion. I looked across the Sound and admired the distant, flashing sight of the old stacks of the Long Island Lighting Company in Northport. Inspired by that glimpse I told the woman I would savor my return journey that night. She replied before I could elaborate on my statement:

"I'm sorry you have such a long ride home," she said.

"No, that's not what I mean at all. This night is so wonderful that the ride delays, defers my—"

"Return to your world," she inserted.

"Yes," I replied, for hers seemed an astounding statement, even if it did not quite represent my meaning. She had landed harder than I on a mutually occupied plank of that boardwalk, its wood rendered as into ivory by the moon.

Humiliations to the Proud

Perhaps it will seem regrettable that, because of my own training as a pianist, I report that I cannot hear the piano playing of myself or others as just music, for the pure sound triggers all my mechanical remembrances of the requirements to produce such sound. But therein lies a hint to a progression of thought that has matured into my perception, my consciousness, of the entire world.

Let me start, however, by explaining my conviction that a vast and undescribed framework for such extra-musical consciousness is suggested by a very fundamental, pedantic, and mechanical aspect of practicing the piano. It is common to advise even the earliest beginners to practice one hand at a time, but let me explore the implications of practicing a very particular kind of keyboard texture with one hand at a time. Take, for example, the final movement of J. S. Bach's G-Major Toccata, a fugue in three voices. Even for a complete layman to follow my analogy, all that is required is that one realize that this is a piece of keyboard music that follows the course of three very independent lines of music—each line of which could be sung by an individual singer: a soprano for the highest part, a bass for the lowest, and an alto, for the middle part. One can imagine that the keyboard texture assigns the highest part to the right hand and the lowest part to the left hand. For the most part this is so. But to which hand is the middle part, the alto, assigned? The answer is that the burden of the middle line is shared by both hands in a very carefully planned choreography designed principally by the composer. Therefore, when one employs the idea of practicing such a texture with only one hand at a time, some very curious and illusory musical effects can be the result, along with, again, some very rarefied extra-musical implications.

To start, how might one describe the strictly musical effects of practicing such a texture with one hand at a time? Imagine a river with continuous curves, incessant bends, the course of which would suggest the illustration of a waveform if seen on a map. Imagine that a kingdom has decided to employ this river as a strict boundary of separation between two municipalities. However, the

mapmakers decide that the boundary is to be a
straight line, a strict line of latitude, that straddles
the average center between the outermost edges of
the curves of the river, instead of in the center of
the devious course of the river itself. If one were
then obliged to limit one's kayaking, say, to only
one municipality's parts of the river, one would
then only be able to paddle in segments of the
river, and memories (that would remind one that
the bends in which one paddles are sourced in part
by convex incursions from the opposite region)
would begin to fade in favor of the false impression
that the edge of the divided kingdom to which one
is confined is lined on its border instead by a series
of thin, segmented, crescent lakes. An otherwise
unsegmented river would soon take on the impression of a series of disconnected cul-de-sacs. The
analogy above begins to suggest the segmentation
that the middle voice of a three-part texture would
suffer when one practices, say, just the left hand
of the final movement of Bach's G-Major Toccata.

Whilst practicing the left hand alone, a pianist would feel in his left hand's outer fingers,
from the unsegmented bass line, an unimpeded
course—as of an unimpeded river deep within its

own, undivided, sovereign territory—but the pianist may begin to feel, in a tactile and, at last, aural sense, that the alto in the middle is nothing but those watery segments of cul-de-sacs I describe above. The pianist might say that practicing this way starts to impress upon the hand and ear a gerrymandered, homophonic misapprehension of the music itself.

But such a misapprehension cannot last long, for wondrous forces cannot be resisted that will not only disabuse one of the illusion of cul-de-sacs but will also suggest degrees of extra-musical consciousness at which I have already begun to hint. If the pianist practicing a Bachian texture with his left hand alone is, again, like that kayaker who remains strictly bound to the false crescent lakes on one side of a divided kingdom—and even if he portages over the gaps in the stream created by the land necessarily intervening between the bends in the false crescents—nothing will stop those fragments of the river from, at last, revealing an undivided current to his hand!

Even without his ear, the hand of the pianist will, at last, sense this. For all the while he plies the creative misreadings of the false cul-de-sacs his other, omitted, hand gains the hoarded strength of a member forced to affect and bide a spurious and unendurable identity as a phantom limb. A pressure to disavow the false separation of left and right leads to a joy of reunion that a higher consciousness such as Bach's can, perhaps, never enjoy because it is without the mortal pianist's, the common man's, limitations. Could one such as a Bach, who never needed to separate the two sides of himself, see the grand implications that can come from the creative misreadings, the one-handed cul-de-sacs, of a musical consciousness inferior to his own?

That progression of creative misreading proceeds as follows: From omitted hand to active hand, there is an incursion of completion that keeps alive all that is omitted. The next leap: a pianist who thinks in such terms begins to think of his entire person as sort of wandering, personified, extra-musical and active hand, who because all piano sound cues his own physical memory, reacts to the piano sound of others, of all other hands, as if it were his own, as if from an omitted part of himself. This second leap is not one of mad, ego-tistical, appropriation, but a progression toward an ultimate sense of awareness that, at last, allows one to hear, see, taste, touch, smell all external events, sense all convex incursions into his life, as if they were but the echo from his own hand's initiatory concave incursion upon the keyboard of Cosmos.

Set a thoughtful child to practicing a Bach fugue one hand at a time, and he will come to feel as if he is living in all his extra-musical time as if within a sphere, the interior lining of which is embroidered as if with an infinite keyboard mechanism. For even when we isolate a hand from the other side of our own self, even when we attempt to further isolate the self from otherness by paring down into a half, into fractions, we cannot escape the convex incursions of the complementary Cosmos.

Thus, with the above reasoning, when I hear any sound from the Cosmos, feel any kind of human sensations from the kickback, as if from the resetting of the hammers, of the action of the figurative universal Klavier, does it not stand to reason that I must have depressed the keys first? I am witness to a creation that is also somehow a reaction to my initiation. I precede the things that inspire me. Or when I lie on my back in the grass at night,

I move my hand toward the points of constellations—toward stars so distant that perhaps they are no longer there—and in occluding collections of these orbs with depressions of my fingers, anticipate a kickback from these ivory points, a reply confirming that I may precede the Cosmos though I be its child. Or as I go about my business here on earth, forming my homophonic misconceptions from practicing the Toccata's fugue with only my left hand, the right hand of the stars compels a reuniting complement. One way or another I build callouses from touching suns.

But, again, I contend that the consequence of such thinking leads, at last, away from ego; it leads toward conscience. Set a child to practicing Mr. Bach one hand at a time, and he cannot fail as a man to read the following of Mr. Emerson as gospel: "Nature and literature are subjective phenomena; every evil and every good thing is a shadow which we cast. The street is full of humiliations to the proud. As the fop contrived to dress his bailiffs in his livery and make them wait on his guests at table, so the chagrins which the bad heart gives off as bubbles, at once take form as ladies and gentlemen in the street, shopmen or bar-keepers in hotels, and threaten or insult whatever is threat-enable and insultable in us."

I have given off such bubbles, and I have seen one take form as a gentleman in the street. Not long ago, when I was away from my native New York and in Los Angeles, I considered carrying out the impulse of reaching out by a hotel phone into my romantic past, to recall a lost romance only so as to hear again the outgoing message of a cell-phone to which I used to place calls every day. It was a childish impulse, and I blush to reveal it, but I must make the confession in order to tell the tale. I knew that a call from California would protect my identity, but I thought better of it. Yet the idea lingered. Some days later, while driving in Connecticut, I stopped at a rest stop, and before leaving the car, I took out some coins from a bag I keep in the car—maybe one quarter, perhaps two, but mostly dimes—just in case there was a pay-phone in the roadside store. I was relieved when I found no payphone. Yet the idea still lingered. On a busy Friday at the end of that same week, I was in New York's Pennsylvania Station. I noted to myself as I passed a payphone that I still had the coins in my jacket's pocket. I resolved to make the call, for though it would not be from out of state, it would still be from an anonymous and unfamiliar area code. I squeezed the talismanic quarter in my pocket and clasped, too, to my resolution, and I kept the payphone in sight as I bought my subway fare for the 1 train.

I heard a voice as I engaged my credit card with the ticket machine for the subway. I thought I had understood plainly what the man had asked (and I had), but I had difficulty believing that the question could have been directed to me; for then the question would seem laden with fantastic, impossible, private knowledge. Because of the extreme itineracy of all people in a great, metropolitan train station, the sudden approach of a vocal stranger in such a place can seem like an apparition to me.

But as I finished my transaction with the machine, the question was asked again, and it was directed unquestionably to me:

"Do you have a quarter?" The question came from a forlorn and derelict looking man. He had a mound of pennies and small coins in his hand. He was trying to work the machine immediately to my side.

"I do," I replied. I reached into my pocket and found the possibly sole quarter amidst the many dimes in my pocket. I handed the man the quarter. He then tried to hand me twenty-five pennies in exchange. I told him it was not necessary, for I realized that two hands had been reunited already and that it was unnecessary for me to make my telephone call.

Praise of God in Solitude

When I was in high school, a few classmates stood behind me in the open doorway of a claustral and windowless practice room that contained a concert grand piano. These young fellows—all students of music, but not one a student of the piano—looked over my shoulder while I played to them from the Paderewski edition of Chopin's nocturnes. One observant member of the group stopped me and challenged my reading of the score. Was I not violating many of the brief but notated rests, and unduly prolonging notes of short duration, by depressing the damper pedal (the piano's rightmost pedal, which activates a mechanism that permits all of the piano's strings to vibrate and thus sound freely) at the same time that I took such care to observe with my fingers those rests and notes of short duration?

I read to my challenger from the remarks at the back of the score: "The pedal marks given by the Editorial Committee are strictly in accordance with the manuscripts and original editions." This argued that the contradiction my fellow student had discovered should be attributed to the composer. I read further to him from the same editorial notes: "In any case, the use of the pedal is a very delicate and entirely individual matter, depending on many factors, such as instrument, touch, tempo or acoustics of the room." In other words, the contradictions he had observed could be extended beyond those called for by Chopin. It was, indeed, an "entirely individual matter." By the time of the 1830s, a pianist engaging the piano's damper pedal for a protracted time while at the same time manually observing rests and notes of brief duration practiced a contradiction that was not a hypocrisy.

This did not satisfy my challenger at all. At last, I could not resist agreeing with my classmate. Because for centuries now notation on the staff has remained so frequently in conflict with coinciding notation for the damper pedal (and in conflict with the damper pedal's use persisting as an "entirely individual matter"), I have, since high school, spent decades suspecting that an elusive and perhaps extra-musical meaning lurks in the preservation of this contradiction. Indeed, something more than musical values must fuel the preservation of this incongruity, for I have rarely encountered a musician or pianist who has found it strange that since the early nineteenth-century, composers of piano music have continued to take the greatest care in notating rests and durations, and to expect that a player will observe those markings with painstaking faithfulness with the fingers, only then to expect the same player to contradict those markings by use of the damper pedal—to the extent that the result could cause even the most accomplished aural transcriber (out of sight of the score and the performer's hands) to render a very different representation in notation than that of the composer's original.

This mystery can be detected from the start of one's study of the piano. After a teacher is certain that a beginning pupil will endeavor first to maintain legato (connectivity from note to note) with the fingers, the pedal is introduced to the student, almost as a reward. An observant beginner will soon note that a sort of reckless legato is a byproduct of the damper pedal's use, yet use of the damper pedal just as quickly hints at hosts of ulterior consequences and mysterious intimations. Notes seem less connected, one to the other, by the damper pedal's use than made to overlap, an overlapping like that one sees relating shingles on a roof: an adjacency so extreme it starts to form mutual occupations of space if not incipient verticalities. When applying the damper pedal to a note, one is reminded that Plato defines a line to be a flowing point. But points made to flow do not provide connectivity between flowing points—no more than do the long June shadows serve, in the forest at the golden hour, to connect solidly the trees; the squirrels cannot rely on those shadows to bridge their journeys from trunk to trunk. They must leap, notwithstanding the false bridges of the shadows, mindful still of the actual gulfs remaining, or claw from adjacent and neighboring branches with the care and caution of a fingered legato.

I begin to ask the seemingly unanswerable: Where in my life beyond the piano, with the activation of a figurative damper pedal, do I encourage, say, a previously articulated sound to cover the care I then take to observe a subsequent silence? Where else do I permit figurative damper pedals to stand as if for body language's role transformed redundantly to sound? Where else, in any arena, do I activate figurative damper pedals? Where else do I sense this contradiction?

JACK KOHL

The answer may lie in an extra-musical sphere, at last, but the solution still remains within the realm of sound. There is a window just out of sight of the desk where I now write these lines. When that window is open but hidden from my eyes, I am reminded through my ears alone of my interest in the sound of a distant radio on a summer day: a sound depleted of all resonance. I experience a similar fascination for that effect when I note the background sound of a radio on a beach, just before the attack on the Kitner boy in the film *Jaws*. When eating recently in an acoustically dry pizza parlor, I could hear Elvis Presley's recording of "Blue Suede Shoes" sounding, at a low volume, behind the chatter in the restaurant. The conditions had robbed the performance of its recorded resonance, of the ambient sound of the space in which the recording had been made. But perhaps most of all, hearing acoustic music performed in the complete absence of ambience, under a dry and open sky, triggers my belief that the first clue in the resolution of the great contradiction is then presented to me. I suspect that even the first reverberant auditoriums were created, not to shield us from the inclemency of actual wetness, but from the aural dryness I cite just above, and then the piano's damper pedal makes the pianist an architect of a still greater reverberance than that enwrapping the performer in such resonant spaces. The damper pedal thus doubles, triples, quadruples the resonant chambers around the thinking performer—the parenthetical depth depending solely on the courage exercised through the performer's right foot. This external parenthetical resonance stands, then, as an emblem for a still greater (and, at last, infinite) parenthetical resonance: the Parenthetical Consciousness that lies within the performer's mind. Thus the longer the external damper pedal is activated, the more the ceaselessly growing concentricity of the player's Parenthetical Consciousness is revealed. How do I define the Parenthetical Consciousness? It is that natural state of private consciousness that is as a piano with dampers always raised.

That consciousness grows for as long as its mortal span permits, but it is contained within a performer who still must honor rests (silences), durations, and articulations in the world outside of that inner consciousness. Even when I am standing, and away from the piano, I catch myself raising my right foot in emblematic gestures, and thus signal my conclusion to keep appointments, honor boundaries and sequence, respect silences, and observe Ten Commandments. Culture and conscience demand intermittent lifting of the right foot. But notwithstanding the care and punctuality of our outward hands upon all actual and figurative keyboards, to the Parenthetical Consciousness it is, again, as if a sort of damper pedal is always activated and dampers are always raised, and thus one is tardy and timely, lawless and lawful, at once within.

Yet at all times the Parenthetical Consciousness dares the actual right foot to lengthen activation of the external damper pedal. And thus from the application of the damper pedal to the dry and careful print of the hands comes a palimpsest of cursive. My right foot in all hours is as an agent transfixed with a reckoning between the external and the internal.

Think of the implications, then, of this scenario: I have been told on good authority that once, as part of a lesson, Vladimir Horowitz pedaled for a gifted student while the latter played, only with his hands, Liszt's *Bénédiction de Dieu dans la Solitude*. I submit that this ostensible division of labor still

had one hearing the full consciousness of Horowitz. And then one is led to wonder, in four-hand
duets at one piano, is not the one who is pedaling
an entirety who is masquerading as a half? One can
only praise God in solitude.

The longer I hold down the damper pedal, it
is as the longer I sit between two mirrors that
face and reflect endlessly the other: the pedaled
sound I produce a reflection of my Parenthetical
Consciousness; my Parenthetical Consciousness
reflecting in turn my pedaled outer sound. Yet I am
never crowded off of the bench by the accumula-
tions of infinity. As Emanuel Swedenborg observes
in *A Treatise Concerning Heaven and Its Wonder, and
Also Concerning Hell:* "The more angels, the more
room."

The longer I depress the damper pedal, I proj-
ect outward in an increasingly degree my Parenthetical Consciousness' concurrent wrestlings and
quick reconciliations with the piece then in performance: all other realizations of tempi, all recol-
lected wrong notes (of which one grows fond and
fascinated), large parallel sections and textures
that reappear in different keys, past parts and
parts yet unplayed, parts of past performances,

even other pieces and experiences; all this heard by the Parenthetical Consciousness in an involuntary and non-sequential manner whilst one endeavors to render a perfect sequence with the fingers. The damper pedal then renders a high burlesque of the player's insides escaping outward. With the hand we maintain a hold on the sequential in all things measurable. With the pedal we engage in a wondrous contradiction against such things. Activation of the damper pedal perpetuates not only all the notes sounded by the player via the keys since the pedal's depression, but also, latently, all of the notes of the piano, and thus all of the notes that have already been played and have yet to be played. Even when playing no notes at all, at the moment of the activation of the damper pedal one hears a subtle but audible, hushed and whiskery, pan-register *zing* from all of the piano's strings. Thus, as the Parenthetical Consciousness basks in a freedom from sequence within, activation of the pedal serves as its mirror and reveals the vulnerability of the ostensibly rigid sequence of any score, and thus of all external events—and suggests that it may raise the veil of threat from all destructive aspects of cause and effect.

Thus, as well, pedaling becomes a lampoon of the art of practicing, for it reveals, to a degree, that the cleaner we play with the fingers, the less we represent our inner selves. Our practicing can then start to seem a madness, as if we endeavor to hide our consciousness by the most careful renderings of the hand. We clean so vigorously and harshly in our practicing, in fact, it is as if we thereby engender scratches in the windows that look inward, and we make them increasingly opaque by reinforcement of our polishing. Yet depress the damper pedal and throw open these windows!

But what prevents us from unremittingly depressing the damper pedal? Why lift and reset its effect so often in performance? Imagine, say, the pianist as a sort of locomotive with an ever-growing *consist* of cars both ahead and behind: endless tenders of Parenthetical Consciousness trailed and pushed at once. I think of this when I ride the Long Island Railroad and approach Jamaica Station, for at the approach to the platform is a placard with a warning for the engineer: *CHECK CONSIST SIZE*. Do we check our own *consist size* when we lift the damper pedal before an audience, for fear that the length of our Parenthetical Consciousness will outstretch the passenger platform and thus baffle any fellow man who can never board most of the train we present?

But I do not think it is in reaction to one's listeners that one, at last, repeatedly depresses and releases the damper pedal in a performance. One feels compelled to follow this cycle even in solitude. Why?

We depress the pedal and raise the dampers (and thus create the contradiction against the work of our mortal hands) in honor of our inner glimpse of a Godly blur of Omniscience. But God lowers dampers at last on our Parenthetical Consciousness, so as to protect us from reaching Impersonality and its stasis, the price of his fully realized Omniscience. Thus we depend on death for the character of our very lives.

When we raise the pedal and thus lower the dampers in our own playing, it is so as to pay homage to this gift of mortality from God, this gift that grants the further gift that God cannot recover for himself: Personality, and thus singular point of view, and thus the gift of mystery which inspires a finite individual toward the assembly of metaphors. Is it a coincidence that the sign given often in a score for the lifting of the damper pedal is an asterisk, a little and mortal star?

It fascinates me that one can practice on a piano if the damper pedal is broken in such a way that the dampers cannot be raised with the pedal. This hints to me that we cherish mortality and character more than we know. For I have never known myself to tolerate practicing on a piano if the damper pedal is broken in such a way that the dampers cannot be lowered. We leave the latter to God.

God is as an organist who sleeps with his brow and limbs draped across the ever-sounding manuals in heaven. He leaves us awake for the mortal day in the nursery below, with the engaging rattle of the piano in our little fingers, but for us to put our foot down should we wish to peek on our guardian in the loft.

About the Author

Jack Kohl is a pianist and author living in the greater New York City area. He is the author of THE PAUKTAUG TRILOGY: *That Iron String, Loco-Motive,* and *You, Knighted States;* and *Bone Over Ivory* and *From the Windows of Diligence,* collections of essays.

Printed in Great Britain
by Amazon